In the fairytale treasury which has come into the world's common possession, there is no doubt that Hans Christian Andersen's stories are of outstanding character. Their symbolism is loaded with Christian values, and some of them are direct illustrations of the gospel. From his early childhood in the town of Odense, Denmark, until his death in Copenhagen, Hans Christian Andersen (1805-1875) had a valid Christian faith which came to expression in many of the approximately 150 stories and tales he wrote. In one of them, he states: "In every human life, whether poor or great, there is an invisible thread that shows we belong to God." The thread in Andersen's stories is one of optimism which has given hope and inspiration to people all over the world.

It is in this spirit the Scandinavia Fairy Tales are published. We are convinced of the validity of teaching spiritual principles and building character values through imaginative stories, just as Jesus used parables to teach the people of his time.

IT'S ABSOLUTELY TRUE
By Hans Christian Andersen
Translated from the original Danish text by Marlee Alex
Illustrated by François Crozat
Published by Scandinavia Publishing House,
Nørregade 32, DK-1165 Copenhagen; Denmark
Text:©Copyright 1984 Scandinavia Publishing House
Artwork:©Copyright 1984 François Crozat and
Scandinavia Publishing House
Printed in Italy

ISBN 87 87732 63 7

It's Absolutely True!

Hans Christian Andersen
Translated from the original Danish text
by Marlee Alex
Illustrated by François Crozat
Scandinavia Publishing House

"It's a shocking story!" said a hen. And it was repeated in a corner of town far from where it originated. "It's a shocking story! It actually happened in a henhouse!" I dare not sleep by myself tonight... good thing we are many here on the roost!" And she began to recount the details so that the feathers on the other hens stood on end; and the cock's comb hung down to the side. It's absolutely true!

4

But let us begin at the beginning: in a henhouse on the other side of town. As the sun set, the hens flew up on their perches. One of them; a white, shortlegged hen who could be counted on to lay her daily egg; was, for a hen, quite respectable on all accounts. As she came to roost she fluffed her feathers with her beak, and a little feather fell out.

"There went that one!" she said. "Of course the more I primp, the nicer I'll look!" And it was said with a tone of jest for she had the best sense of humor among all the hens, in addition to being respectable as I have already mentioned. Then she fell asleep. It was dark all around.

The hens sat side by side; and the one which sat closest to her couldn't sleep. She listened as though she wasn't listening, as one should do in this world in order to live peacefully. But she couldn't help saying to her neighbor on the other side: "Have you heard? I won't mention names but one of the hens intends to pluck out her feathers hoping to become good looking. If I were the cock I would hate her."

And just above the hens sat the owl with her owl husband and owl children. They had sharp ears, and they heard every word which the neighbor hen had said. They rolled their eyes and the owl mother fluttered her wings.

"Don't listen! But you did hear that, didn't you? I heard it with my own ears, and they must hear a lot before they fall off! One of the hens has, to a certain degree forgotten what is proper for a hen. She sits and plucks her feathers out, and allows the cock to watch!"

"Prenez garde aux enfants!" said the owl husband. "It is not a story for the children to hear!"

"Indeed! I'm going to tell the owl next door! She is the most highly regarded owl around." And the mother owl flew away.

13

"Who – who! Uwhoooo!" cried the both of them right down to the doves below. "Have you heard! Have you heard! Uwhooo! One of the hens has plucked out all her feathers for the sake of the cock! She'll freeze to death if she hasn't already. Uwhooo!"

"Where, where?" cooed the doves. "In the chickenyard next door! I have just as well as seen it myself. It's almost too improper to repeat it! But it's absolutely true!"

"True, true; believe every word!"
said the doves as they cooed down
to the hen-house below them.
"There is a hen, and some say there
are two; who have plucked out all
their feathers so they won't look like
the others, hoping to gain the
attention of the cock! What a daring
thing to do; one could catch a cold
or die of fever; and the both of them
are dead!"

"Wake up! Wake up!" Crowed the cock as he flew up on the fence. He still had sleep in his eyes, but he crowed anyway: "There are three hens who have died because they were lovesick for a rooster. They plucked out all their feathers. It's a disgusting story, I don't care to keep it, pass it on!"

"Pass it on!" squeaked the bats. And the hens cackled and the cock crowed: "Pass it on! Pass it on!" And so the story was passed from henhouse to henhouse until, at last, it returned to the place where it started.

"There are five hens," it was said, "who have plucked out all their feathers in order to prove which had grown the thinnest out of lovesickness for a rooster. And then they pecked each other to death much to their shame, as well as the disgrace of their families, and to the great loss of their owner."

And the hen from which the little feather had fallen could not, of course, recognise her own story. And since she was a respectable hen, she said, "I loathe hens like those. But there are plenty of their kind! Such things shouldn't be kept a secret.

I will do everything I can to get this story printed in the newspaper so it can be spread over the whole countryside. Those hens deserve as much, and their families with them!"

21

And it appeared in the newspaper, printed for all to see, and it's absolutely true: one little feather can easily become five hens.

Explaining the story:

From the story of the hen who lost a feather we learn how rumours get started and how unkind talk about the affairs of other people can make small events seem bigger and can even create disgraceful stories which have no basis in fact.

Talking about the truth of the story:

1. What happened actually to the first hen?
2. Retell in your own words how the story was changed till it finally ended up in the paper.
3. What did the neighbour hen do to start the unkind story rolling?
4. As the story became bigger and bigger, what kind of problems do you think it might have created in the barnyard?
5. What does the Bible say about our tongue? See James 3:5. (Also Proverbs 11:9, 11:13 and 18:8).

Applying the truth of the story:

1. Do you think it might have been better if the neighbour hen kept quiet and avoided making any negative comment about the first hen? Why?
2. How could the story have been stopped somewhere along the way?
3. How do you react when you hear unkind things about other people which you know may not be true?
4. What can we do to keep gossip from spreading? See Philippians 4:8.